The

RAGGY
TAGGY
TOYS

THIS BOOK DONATED BY:

Rachel De Ieso

The

RAGGY
TAGGY
TOYS

Joyce Dunbar · Pictures by P. J . Lynch

BARRON'S

New York · Toronto

For Sylvia, Emily and Molly
J. D.

For my parents, Anna and Liam
P. J. L.

First edition for the United States and Canada
published 1988 by Barron's
Educational Series, Inc.
Text copyright © Joyce Dunbar 1988
Illustrations copyright © Patrick James Lynch 1988
First published 1988 by
Orchard Books
London England

All inquiries should be addressed to:
Barron's Educational Series, Inc.
250 Wireless Boulevard
Hauppauge, New York 11788

Library of Congress Catolog Card No 88-14674

International Standard Book No. 0-8120-4130-5
Library of Congress Cataloging-in-Publication Data
Dunbar. Joyce.
The raggy taggy toys/Joyce Dunbar: pictures by P.J. Lynch. — —
1st ed. for the United States.
p.   cm.
Summary: When Hannah's mother tries to clear away Hannah's
collection of raggy old toys, she gets a big surprise.
ISBN 0-8120-4130-5
[1. Toys-Fiction. 2. Magic-Fiction.] I. Lynch, Patrick James,
ill. II Title.
PZ7. D8944Rag 1988
[E]— — dc 19 88-14674 CIP AC 88-14674

Printed in Belgium by Proost
890 987654321

Once there was a little girl who loved raggy toys. Her name was Hannah Hubbard, and she was very kindhearted.

One day she found a scruffy knitted rabbit in a muddy puddle.

"You poor rabbit," she said, shaking the wet off his ears. She tucked him under her arm and carried him all the way home, where there were lots of other scruffy toys that nobody wanted but Hannah.

Some had followed her home from garage sales.

Some had climbed out of old toy drawers where they'd been left and long forgotten.

Some had even escaped from the trash cans!

"Hannah will give us a home," they said to each other. And they were right. She always did.

Hannah loved her toys and knew them each by name. There was Slamerkin, the donkey, Gabby, the flat rag doll, Snicker-Snack, the crumpled cloth crocodile, and Boggin and Droop, who didn't know what they were.

And now there was Sprinkle, the knitted rabbit. He was cleaned and washed and dried, but sprinkling sawdust everywhere, through a tiny hole in his toe.

There were many more besides.

Hannah told them secrets and she sang them songs. The toys kept all the secrets and they listened to the songs.

They were all very happy.

But sometimes, on some days, one person
wasn't happy at all. . .
    Hannah's mother!

Her name was Mrs. Isabel Hubbard. Once she had been a little girl called Izzie, but that was a long time ago, and she'd forgotten all about it.

Now she was a mother and housewife.

She loved her little girl and so she tried to put up with the toys, but she didn't like the housework one bit! She fretted and frowned and got into a terrible mood.

"Down-at-heel draggletail!" she would shout at Dusty, the patchwork mouse.

"Horrible rag-tag!" she called Clod-hop, the corduroy clown.

And though the toys kept quiet, they were very much offended.

Hannah did her best to make the toys change their ways, so that her mother wouldn't mind them so much.

"Sit up straight," she said, smoothing them down and propping them up. "Stay in a neat row."

But it did no good. The toys soon flopped down again. They simply could not help it, not even to please Mrs. Hubbard.

The sawdust was the very last straw.

Hannah's mother found it. . . and followed it. . . until she came to Sprinkle, with the hole in his toe.

"I've had enough!" she scolded. "I'm getting rid of every one of you!"

Throwing them into a pile Mrs. Hubbard started singing:

"I'm going to get rid of this rabble
I'm going to chuck out this mob
Don't dilly, don't dally, don't dabble
Just stick to the the job!"

Poor Hannah was in tears. "But *where* are you sending them?" she cried.

"To the Back of Beyond," snapped her mother, going off to get a sack.

Now it so happened that the toys knew more about the Back of Beyond than Mrs. Hubbard did, because they had been there, once before. What's more, *they* knew the way.

With a nod and a wink to each other, they stacked themselves up against the door.

When Hannah's mother tried to get back into the room, she found that the door wouldn't budge. She pushed, and she pulled, then she pushed really hard, until suddenly the toys all scattered!

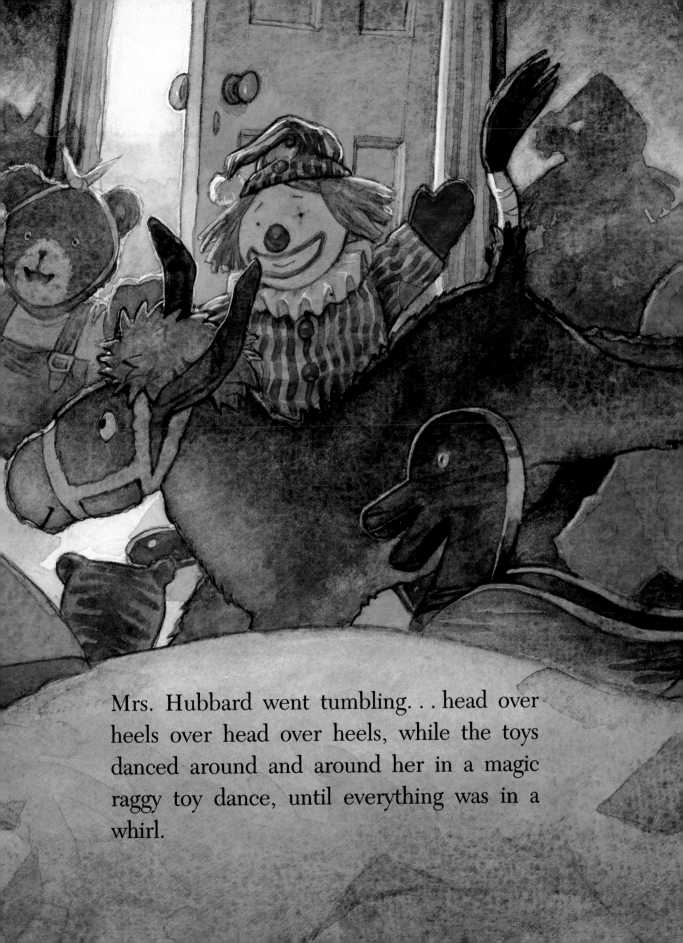

Mrs. Hubbard went tumbling. . . head over heels over head over heels, while the toys danced around and around her in a magic raggy toy dance, until everything was in a whirl.

Then slowly things became still.

"Where am I?" said Mrs. Hubbard, for everything around looked strange.

She stood at the top of some stairs. . . with nowhere to go but down.

Dusty took away her broom.

Gabby took away her feather duster.

Clod-hop took away her mop.

While down she went and down, growing lighter and lighter. . . smaller and smaller. . . younger and younger. . . so that by the time she reached the bottom. . .

she was a little girl again!

"Hello, Izzie," called lots of toys. "Welcome to the Back of Beyond."

"Wherever's that?" she asked.

"The Back of Beyond is where forgotten
things are," said Snicker-Snack. "It's where
we play games to help us remember."
And they did.

They played raggle-taggle tig
And danced a ragamuffin jig
They did the scallywag hop
Until Izzie said, "Stop!
Where's Suzie, my button-eyed doll?"

"Not here," said Boggin, "so she can't be quite forgotten."

"And where's Hannah, my little girl?"

"Not here," said Droop, "so she can't be forgotten either."

"Of course she's not forgotten," said Izzie. "So why don't we get her to play?"

And without looking to see if they followed her, Izzie started back up the stairs. Up and up she climbed, so fast and so excited that she was soon out of breath and her head was in a whirl.

And she was Mrs. Hubbard again, in Hannah's room, with the raggy-taggy toys all around her.

"Mom! Mom! What's the matter?" asked Hannah, tugging at her sleeve.

"I'm not sure," said Mrs. Hubbard, with a dreamy smile. "I just felt a little dizzy. But it made me remember someone. Just you wait here a minute."

Soon Mrs. Hubbard was back, with a button-eyed doll in her hands. A raggy-taggy button-eyed doll!

"This is Suzie," she said. "She used to be mine. Now she can be yours."

Hannah gave her mother a great big hug.

"Oh, thank you, Mom," she said.

Then together they fixed up the toys. Sprinkle had his toe sewn up, and to make Suzie feel really at home, they all had a lovely snack.

WAKEFIELD ELEMENTARY
SCHOOL

DATE DUE	BORROWER'S NAME	ROOM NUMBER
11-13	Rachel DeIeso	
11-24		
3-5	Joanne	K-Am
4-10	Joseph F	K-Am
11/17	Micah	2P
1-8	Jessica P	2P
1-15	Jennifer	2D